...ne Perry

Rose
Between
Two Thorns

A Timepiece Novel

LONDON BOROUGH OF WANDSWORTH	
9030 00002 9481 6	
Askews & Holts	29-Nov-2012
JF TEENAGE 11-14	£6.99
	WWX0010241/0040

First published in 2012 in Great Britain by
Barrington Stoke Ltd
18 Walker Street, Edinburgh, EH3 7LP

www.barringtonstoke.co.uk

ISBN: 978-1-84299-908-0

Printed in China by Leo

Contents

Chapter 1

Dignity

A woman in a white cap and a red cloak watched from the crowd as the tall, thin man walked out onto the wooden platform. It was a dark, windy day, and the man's grey hair blew out from under his tall black hat. As he passed across the platform, a small girl ducked between the men and women in the crowd, ran forward and reached up to touch his feet.

The tall man stopped in front of a shorter man with fair hair. They spoke for a moment and then the tall man turned away. He took off his black hat, his rings and the medal round his neck and passed them to a third man, who wore the white collar of a priest. Then he tied a white cap over his hair and went down on his knees in front of the block.

Under the stage, the small girl watched the axe rise into the air. As it fell, bright red blood splashed down on her face.

"And that's all it took," said Mr Jones. As the lights came on, the screen stayed frozen on the shot of the girl with her face covered in blood.

The class blinked and shifted as they came back to the here and now. Many still stared at the girl on the screen.

"Just one axe blow," Mr Jones carried on, "and King Charles I was dead. It was 1649 and Oliver Cromwell and his New Model Army were in charge. England would never be the same again." He turned and looked at the class. "Let's see ..." he said. "Stacey, what did you think of the film?"

Stacey Summers screwed up her nose. "Call that a film?" she asked. "Give me a bit of hot vampire action any day."

A few other girls sniggered and one of the boys gave a wolf whistle.

Mr Jones shook his head. "Witty as ever, Stacey," he said. "Let's try someone else. How about you, Rosie? What did you make of it?"

"It was good," Rosie said. "It was like you could feel how upset the people in the crowd were. And the man who played the King was fantastic. He made you feel so sorry for him. He had such ... dignity, even when he was going to die."

"You're right, Rosie," Mr Jones said. "King Charles did die with dignity. And many people did feel sorry for him. We must remember, class, that a lot of people in 1649 didn't want their King to be put on trial, and for many, many more the idea of *killing* a king was terrible. That's why Oliver Cromwell stopped a lot of MPs from going into Parliament when the vote was cast. He kept the ones away who would never agree to a trial." The history teacher smiled at Rosie. "Thank you for your input, Rosie. Well done."

For the rest of the lesson, Rosie felt like Stacey's eyes were burning holes in her back. She knew that Stacey would be furious. It was bad enough that Rosie had stopped being her friend and mucking about with her in class, but now she had gone and showed Stacey up in front of Mr Jones. Stacey had a nasty side, and Rosie was worried about what she would do to get her own back. When the bell went for Break, Rosie hung about at her desk putting her pens and books away in her bag. She wanted to put off going out into the corridor for as long as she could, in the hope that Stacey would have gone.

No such luck. As Rosie stepped out of the classroom, she heard Stacey say something about 'dignity' and then there was a burst of sniggering from the gang of friends she always had with her. Rosie kept her head down and went to walk past.

"You know that Rosie can't read, don't you?" Stacey asked her friends, in a loud voice so Rosie could hear. "Must have made it so much easier for her, having that video to watch today."

"What are you talking about, Stacey?" said another voice.

Rosie swung her head up in horror. Zack Edwards was coming along the corridor towards her, and he had heard what Stacey had said. Zack was Rosie's friend, maybe even her boyfriend, and Stacey knew that he was the person whose opinion mattered most to Rosie.

"Of course Rosie can read," Zack said, and put an arm round Rosie's waist. "Can't you, Rosie?" he asked, and smiled down at her.

"I – I – I – " Rosie stuttered.

"See?" Stacey said. "Told you she can't. There's something wrong with her, isn't there, Rosie? Poor cow."

Rosie turned on her heel and fled.

Rosie was sitting on the wall behind the school with her head in her hands when she felt a shadow fall across her. She lifted her head far enough to see Zack's green trainers on the ground in front of her, then covered her face again.

"You're not a dog, Rosie," Zack said. "Even if you can't see me, you know I'm here."

Rosie didn't say anything.

"Why didn't you tell me?" Zack asked. "I mean, it's a big thing to keep to yourself." When Rosie didn't answer, he kept on. "I thought you liked me," he said. "In fact, I thought you liked me a lot. Was I wrong? Is that why you didn't tell me?"

"I do like you," Rosie said. "But I knew *you* wouldn't like *me* if you knew I was thick."

"You *are* thick," Zack said. "If that's what you think."

Rosie felt the tears slide down her cheeks but she managed to get a tight little smile onto her face. "Thanks," she said. "Well, at least I know where I stand now. I'm thick, and you're shot of me. Bye, Zack." She stood up and swung her bag over her arm.

"Come on, Rosie! That's not what I said and you know it!" Zack tried to grab hold of her as she passed him, but she twisted out of his grasp and ran off. She heard him shout after her, but she didn't go back. She ran and ran and only stopped when, at last, she was out of breath.

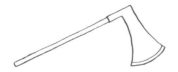

Chapter 2
Confessing

"What's the matter with you?" Rosie's mother demanded as soon as she came in the back door. "You should still be at school." Then she saw the tears on Rosie's cheeks and her face filled with worry. "What's wrong, sweetheart? What's happened?"

Rosie took a deep breath.

"Stacey and some other girls said something about me today at school and everyone heard," she said. "And I fell out with Zack because of it."

"Who's Zack?" her mother asked. "And what did Stacey say?"

"Zack is – was – sort of my boyfriend," Rosie said. "And Stacey told everyone I can't read. So now Zack thinks I'm thick, and so does everyone else."

"But that's just silly," her mother said. "Of course you can read. You learned when you were little."

Rosie's eyes filled with tears again. "No, Mum," she said. "I never learned. The letters just don't make any sense to me. The lady at the library says I've got dyslexia."

"But I don't understand," her mother said. "If you've got that, why didn't anyone tell your father and me? Why didn't *you* tell us?"

Rosie started to cry properly. "I was so ashamed. I thought I was retarded or something. I'm so sorry, Mum!"

"Oh, poor love," her mother said, and put her arms round Rosie. "There, there. There's no need to cry. You've told us now and that's all that matters. I'm not angry. I'm just sorry you didn't tell us. I feel like we've let you down."

When Rosie was calmer, her mum made them both a cup of tea and opened some fancy biscuits she had in the cupboard. They were still chatting at the kitchen table when Rosie's dad came home from work. Rosie tried to go up to her bedroom while her mum told him about the dyslexia, but her mum said not to be so silly.

"Tell him yourself, Rosie," she said. "He'll understand."

And he did. At first he was a bit upset, like her mum, but then he said that Rosie had been very clever to manage to hide such a big thing from them for so long.

"How did you get by in school?" he asked. "It must have been so hard!"

"It was," Rosie said. "For a while I just mucked about with Stacey so everyone would think I just couldn't be bothered. But now I'm getting help and I'm trying hard to do well. I like school a lot."

"I think we should go up to the school on Monday," her father said. "It's not right that they didn't get help for you for so long."

"No, please," Rosie said. "You can come up, but please don't complain. I was such a nightmare in class that they didn't have a chance to notice my reading. And Mr Jones, my history teacher, did try to help. It was because of him that I first started to go to the dyslexia group at the library." *Not only thanks to him*, she thought, but she didn't say anything about Queen Elizabeth I or Edith Cavell or any of the other people who had helped her learn to believe in herself. Her parents would think she was mad if she started claiming to have met people who had been dead for hundreds of years.

"So tell us about this Zack boy, then," her mother said. "Was he mean to you when he found out? He doesn't sound like a very nice lad if he was. I mean, it's not your fault, is it?"

"He said I was ..." Rosie didn't finish her sentence. She had been going to say that Zack had said she was stupid, but now she saw that that wasn't true. She had been so upset that she hadn't listened to him. He had just been upset that she hadn't trusted him enough to tell him. Pretty much like her mum and dad.

Rosie stood up. "You know what?" she said. "Zack wasn't mean to me. But I was so upset that I wouldn't listen when he tried to be nice. If it's OK, I'll go and phone him. I need to say I'm sorry."

She left her mum and dad in the kitchen and ran upstairs to find her phone. Her hands shook as she scrolled down to Zack's number and pressed 'call'. It went straight to voicemail and Rosie remembered that it was Friday – the night Zack's brother always tried to call from his army base in Afghanistan to speak to his family. She left a message to say to call her, her voice a bit shaky, and hung up.

Once that was done she felt a bit better. She lay down on the bed and closed her eyes, dead tired from all the crying. Even though she was still a bit nervous about speaking to Zack, she felt like a weight had been lifted from her. She closed her eyes and listened to her parents potter about in the kitchen below.

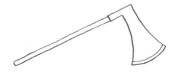

Chapter 3
Back again

Rosie was shaken awake before it was fully light. The first thing she was aware of was how cold she was. Her feet were nearly numb, and no matter how tight she pulled the blankets, there was no real warmth in them. A woman stood over the bed, smiling at her – she wore a long black dress, very plain and with a big white collar.

All of a sudden, the cold mattered a whole lot less. Rosie was in the past again.

"Time to get up, Rose," the woman said in a sweet voice. "There's work to do. Only one more day to go now."

Rosie sat up, shivering in spite of the thick flannel night-dress she was wearing. *Please, no! she thought. Not now! I know I wanted to come back, but not before I'd had a chance to speak to Zack and put things right.*

The woman raised a candle in a metal holder and peered at Rosie. "Are you well, daughter?" she asked.

"Yes," said Rosie, even though she didn't feel well at all. "I think I'm still a little asleep, that's all."

The woman put a cool hand on Rosie's cheek and smiled. Rosie looked at her again. She had no make-up on at all, and her hair was pulled back off her face, no waves, no curls. It made her look unhappy, as if she were not very well.

"Are *you* well, Mother?" Rosie asked.

The woman smiled. "I am, praise God. Now come, Rose. We will break our fast on the hour. You had better hurry."

"Yes, Mother."

Rosie's clothes were on the back of a plain wooden chair. There was a long white petticoat, a grey dress, shoes, thick stockings and a long white apron. With a sigh, Rosie swung her legs out of bed. At least she had learned to tie up dress laces on her other trips to the past.

There was no carpet on the floor, but there was a rag rug. Rosie was glad of it as she shuddered in the cold of the room. She pulled on the clothes and a pair of clumsy, heavy shoes, then poured water from a jug to wash. The water was cold and the shock of it on her skin was almost like being struck. She was glad of the rough cloth of the towel to dry herself.

Downstairs a tall man was standing in a room set out for a meal. Rosie knew this must be her father. His hair was long and he wore very plain clothes, buttoned up to the neck. His breeches reached to just under the knee, and below them were thick stockings and heavy shoes, a bit like Rosie's own.

Rosie bowed her head. "Good morning, Father."

Her father didn't smile. "It is indeed a good morning, Rose," he said. "And tomorrow will see the dawn of a new life in England, praise be to God."

Rosie looked up, not sure of what he meant.

"I see the hope in your face," her father told her. "It pleases me, daughter. Too many young people are given to silliness and lack of proper respect. As soon as your mother returns we shall give thanks to God for our lives and our health and ask His aid in all our doings this day."

Rosie's jaw dropped open. There was a fierce light in this man's eye, a sort of hard, angry joy, but he did not look as if he could smile, let alone laugh. How could Rosie sit and eat with him – and how would she know what to say and do?

Just then the woman came back into the room, her eyes lowered. She stood in silence with her hands folded in front of her. Rosie found herself copying her, as if this were something she was used to doing every day.

Her father began to pray aloud, thanking God for what seemed like everything he could possibly think of. He went on and on, like the worst kind of vicar in church. Rosie found herself praying too – praying that he would stop so she could eat something hot at last.

What was it that made this man tick? He didn't seem to be making himself happy with all this stuff about God. Rosie wanted to look up and watch his face, but she was scared that he might be watching her, and then she would be caught. It might even be some sort of crime to have your eyes open while someone was praying. Rosie thought that was the sort of belief this man had – a belief in a God who didn't actually like people much at all and who would love to catch them doing something wrong.

Chapter 4
A Visitor

After they had eaten, the day's work began
in the family tailor's shop where Rosie's father
made and mended clothes. He was a good tailor.
The clothes were all very simple, of plain wool
in dark colours, but there was an art to cutting
cloaks and jackets so that they fitted, were comfy
and let a person move freely without rubbing
the skin or coming apart. Rosie and her mother
stitched hems and Rosie was pleased when her
mother said how neat Rosie's work was. All that
time helping her grandma to stitch together
knitted squares into blankets hadn't been wasted.

It was early evening when a thin, wiry man came into the shop. At once Rosie's father stopped what he was doing and threw the jacket he was mending down on the bench in front of Rosie. His face lit with joy and he stood up in respect.

Rosie felt she should stand too, although she had no idea why.

"Good to see you, Mr Smith," the man said. "I have a small tear in my sleeve. Would you mend it for me while I wait? I want tomorrow to be perfect in every way. It is the beginning of a new age, glory be to God."

"Of course." Rosie's father took the man's coat with a respect and care that he had shown for no other customer. He peered at the tear and then, instead of asking Rosie to find a thread of the right colour, he went to look for one himself.

Rosie stayed on her feet, staring at the man. Who was he? What had he done to make Rosie's father admire him so? He was normal to look at, with a bony face and eyes that burned like those of a man in a fever.

The man turned to Rosie. "Take up your work, girl. It is a sin to be idle."

"Yes, sir," Rosie said. "Thank you." As fast as she could, she sat down and turned her eyes to her needle. Her cheeks burned.

"What a blessing to be born a girl in this time," the stranger said to Rosie's father. "A girl need not take part in fighting, shed blood, risk being maimed in our battles. But she can grow up in the land we have won – a land under God, and the rule of Lord Protector Cromwell."

"Indeed," said Rosie's father. "Rose will live a life we paid for with blood." He blinked and for an instant Rosie saw that his eyes were full of tears.

The visitor stood up a little and put a hand on Rosie's father's arm. "I forgot, you lost your brother at the siege of Oxford, didn't you?" he said. "But he died in a great cause."

"He did," Rose's father said. "And he was as good a man as you could wish to know. But it is my son I grieve for. He was wounded at Naseby. He lost his leg and might as well have lost his arm too, for all the use it is to him how. It took all the courage he had not to weep from the pain of it. And there's nothing I can do to help him, but see that he is fed and clothed."

"The Man of Blood will pay," the visitor said. "In the court of men tomorrow, and the court of God forever."

"Praise be to God," Rosie's father said. He finished stitching the tear and held it up for the man to see.

"Ah – perfect as always," the man said with a smile. He put the coat on again, and handed over a couple of coins. "Thank you. Be joyful tomorrow. God be with you, and all your house."

Rosie's mind was buzzing so much she could hardly focus on the stitching in front of her eyes. The visitor had talked about Oliver Cromwell, so this must be England at the time of the Civil War. And her father had talked about a son who had been badly hurt in a battle. Where was he? Had Rosie been sent to help him? And why did everyone keep going on about tomorrow?

At least the last question was an easy one to get an answer to.

"Why did that man say we should be joyful tomorrow?" she asked.

"Because tomorrow the King will die," her father said. "And that will be the end of his unjust rule."

"You mean he'll be killed?" Rosie asked. "How can that be good? You're supposed to be a Christian, aren't you? I thought the Bible said it was wrong to kill."

"Not when death is a just punishment for a crime," her father replied. "The King refuses to repent for his sins. He will go to his grave as arrogant as he has been in life. Cromwell will be Lord Protector of England, and the evil deeds and the waste of the King and his court will be over. He was tried before the people, and he was found guilty. This is a great time for England, Rose. Our visitor, Praisegod Barebones, was right. You are blessed to live at such a time. Now go and sit with your brother. Your mother and I can finish here."

Praisegod Barebones? Rosie thought. *Are these people mad?*

21

Chapter 5
David

Rosie woke up in her clean, bare bedroom the next morning just as cold as she had been the morning before. It was the end of January. There was ice in the wind that howled across the roofs and rattled the windows.

This time her mother had not needed to call her. She had woken several times in the night, thinking of all that had happened and wondering what the day would be like. Each time she had opened her eyes and hugged the blankets closer round herself as she remembered her brother

David's white, pained face and the stories he had whispered to her as she sat by his bed.

First he had told her about the battle at Naseby, when a bullet wound in his leg had gone bad and they had had to cut it off. Rosie had seen awful things in Edith Cavell's hospital in World War One, but at least then there had been some medical care. She found it hard to imagine how much pain David must have suffered, with no drugs or doctors to make it better.

After that, David told her about the girl he loved, who had dark hair and a face more lovely than anything he had ever seen. He reached his hand under his pillow and took out a small gold object he had hidden there. Rosie's heart started to beat faster – it was a watch!

"Here she is," David said, and handed Rosie the watch. He had opened the case and she saw that it also held a tiny painting of a young woman with curly dark hair and a pretty smile. But Rosie felt her own smile fade as her hand closed around the watch. It felt cold in her hand, not like the watches that had taken her back to her own time before. They had all been warm, heated by whatever magic let them open time. Somewhere in the back of Rosie's mind an alarm bell began to ring. She had been warned that, unless she could find one of the special watches, she could be stuck in the past forever. *Please*, she thought. *Not here! Not now!*

David had not noticed that Rosie had grown quiet. He was still talking about the girl, whose name was Marie.

"There's something so bright in her face," he said. "And gentle, too. She always looks like she's about to laugh, but also like she cares for people deeply. I've never heard her mock anyone, or make light of someone else's pain."

"I know someone like that," Rosie told him, thinking of Zack and wishing that she had given him a chance when he had come after her yesterday at school. *Yesterday?* she thought, feeling something half-way between panic and a desire to laugh. *If this is 1649, that day won't happen for almost 400 years. If I don't find a watch, I'll die hundreds of years before Zack is even born!* But then Rosie looked at David's pale face as he gazed at the picture in the watch and she told herself not to worry. She had to trust that the right watch would come to her. And it seemed there was something she had to do here, in this time, first.

"Marie's had more than her fair share of grief to carry in the last few weeks," David said. "And tomorrow will be terrible for her."

That was when Rosie understood why Marie could not come to David on his sick-bed, or David go to her. She and her family were Royalists. His father had fought for the King.

"Her father wears such fancy clothes," David was saying. "Velvet coats with lace collars and velvet breeches and leather boots up to his knees. He wears his hair long and curly and has a pointy beard. And Marie wears dresses with lace at the neck, as if she wants the whole world to know she supported the King! I wish she would stop – it could be the death of her!"

David rose up on his good elbow as he spoke of the danger Marie might be in and his pale cheeks flushed red. Rosie jumped up and made him lie back on the pillows.

"Hush, now," she said. "You can't help her if you don't get better yourself."

For a moment David looked like he might argue, but then pain clouded his eyes and he lay back. "You're right," he said, after a moment. "She can't lose me too. Her brother died at

Marston Moor, you know. She loved him so much, she still can't speak of him without tears filling her eyes, even though there have been so many battles and deaths since then. And the King has been caught and put in prison. And will be killed."

"Where's the Queen?" Rosie asked.

"Fled to France," David said, but it was clear he didn't care much about the Queen when he had Marie to worry about.

"Today will be the final defeat for her," he said. "The end of hope for the cause she cares so much about. I wish I could do something, at least say to her that I'm sorry it's ended this way. I hate to think of her left alone, believing no one else cares about her. Her mother is dead. Her father is wrapped up in his own grief, and he doesn't think of how sad and frightened she is too."

"I'll go," said Rosie. "In the morning. If you give me the watch, then I'll know her."

Chapter 6
A Plan

David's face grew light for a moment, then his eyes darkened again. "Father won't let you go," he said.

"Father doesn't need to know," Rosie said. "Tell them I'm ill and I want to be left to sleep. We'll make a pile of clothes in my bed and it will look like I'm lying under the covers. But you'll have to sit by the bed all day and keep Mother out. Can you do that?"

"Yes," said David. "I think I can. Thank you, Rosie!"

And now morning had come. Before she could change her mind, Rosie got up and dressed and then piled David's cloak and clothes under the covers on her bed so it looked like someone was lying there. Then she went to fetch David from his room. The house was freezing and she covered him with more cloaks and blankets while he made himself as comfortable as he could in the chair by the bed where he would pretend to keep watch over her.

At least there is no work today, Rosie told herself as she crept down the stairs. Her parents wouldn't need her and they would be busy with visitors and prayers and the great events of the day. Perhaps they wouldn't insist on getting David back to bed and going into her room.

Outside, the streets were empty and dark. It was not so long after the middle of winter and there would be no light until nearly eight in the morning. Rosie struggled to follow the directions David had given her. She knew that he had gone to Marie's house so often that he could have found his way there blind-folded, but she had no idea where it was.

First light was coming as, at last, Rosie reached the kitchen door of Marie's home and knocked. It was opened within moments by the cook, a large woman who had what should have been a kind, smiley face, but today it was pinched with sorrow.

"What do you want?" she said. "Come to gloat, have you?"

Rosie shook her head. "I came to tell Miss Marie ... " She stopped, not knowing how much she should say to the cook about Marie and David.

"To tell her what?" the cook asked.

In the end, Rosie took out the watch and held it up, hoping that the woman wouldn't be angry. "My brother sent me," she said. "He's Miss Marie's ... friend. He wanted very badly to make sure she was all right. That she wasn't alone today."

The cook looked at the watch for a long second. Her voice was gentler when she spoke again. "Are you David's sister, then, lass?" she asked. "He's a good lad, for a Puritan, and you're a kind sister to come here with a message. But Miss Marie's gone already. Her father's going to walk with the King, and she's gone to watch. I couldn't stop her, poor lamb."

"By herself?" Rosie was appalled.

"Yes," the cook said, and pulled the door open wider. "And she went without a bite inside her. As if starving herself would help the King, poor soul."

"Give me something to take to her," Rosie said.

"Bless you for offering," the cook said. "But you can't. What would your parents say?"

"They don't even know I've gone," said Rosie.

With a smile, the cook took Rosie into the large, warm kitchen. She gave her some hot gruel and Rosie ate it while the cook got some bread and cheese to take to Marie.

"Where did she go?" Rosie asked.

"Whitehall," the cook replied. "But I don't know how you'll find her in the crowds that'll be there later. She's only a slip of a thing, like you. But bless you for trying!"

"I'll find her!" Rosie promised. She took the food the cook had wrapped in a cloth. "I will."

But out in the street, as the thin, winter light grew in the sky and shone on the ice on the roofs

and Rosie slipped and slid along the uneven road,
she wondered if she was being a fool. There was
no way she could change what would happen
today. The King would die, and that would be
that. And what comfort could Rosie offer Marie
when she turned up in her dark Puritan dress
and hat that were symbols of everything Marie
and her family had fought against?

But David loves her, she told herself. *And
perhaps she loves him too.*

Chapter 7

The Shadow of an Axe

As she walked closer to the centre of the city, Rosie passed groups of people huddled together. Some talked in low voices, others in great shouts.

"This is the beginning of a new world!" a thin-lipped man said, with a wild light in his eyes. "There'll be no more lust and vanity."

"Of course there will," someone else said. "They'll be punished, that's all."

"God's punishment," the first man snapped back. "No more running around in vulgar dress, no more crude talk and no more indecent goings-on."

"I don't mind what folks do behind closed doors," an old woman said. "What's it to us if they wear fancy clothes at court, or have dirty pictures on their walls? But there'll be no more taxes that crush us, and laws won't change from one week to the next. That's what matters."

Rosie rushed on. She didn't want anyone to ask her what she thought about it all. All she cared about was an end to war, and to this world in which David and Marie couldn't be together because people loved or hated other people for the side they were on and not for who they were. It was all miserable, and scary. Perhaps the best thing about what was going to happen today wasn't that one side had won, but that the war was over.

Rosie passed more groups of people. This time many of them wore fancy clothes, with long hair, big floppy hats and lace collars. For all their lovely things, their faces were pinched and sad, and one or two of the women were already weeping.

But where was Marie?

Twice Rosie saw girls who might have been her, but both times when she came closer and they turned towards her, their faces were not like the one in the watch and Rosie's heart sank with sudden disappointment.

The crowd all seemed to be moving one way, and Rosie allowed herself to be carried along with them. She asked an old woman where they were and the woman said they were almost at the Palace at Whitehall. This must be where Marie was coming!

Now there were soldiers mixed in the crowd. Rosie remembered from school that Cromwell's men were called the New Model Army. They stood tall and grim, with round metal helmets on their heads and metal armour around their chests and backs. Many of them carried huge pikes with blades on the end which looked like they could cut a man clean in two.

Rosie wondered if any of these men was Oliver Cromwell himself. She was sure he would be here. This was his big moment – his victory. If you had the power and the will to sentence a king to death, surely you would have the stomach to be there when he died?

Rosie looked along the rows of faces, and then realised she would not know Cromwell if she saw him. She had no real idea what he looked like, only an image in her mind of the actor who had played him in the film she had seen in Mr Jones' class.

Just then, though, Rosie thought she saw someone she did know. The man had his back to her, but something about the way he stood made her reach out to him. "Excuse me, sir!" she said. The man turned and Rosie began to smile, but instead of the gentle face and startling blue eyes she had expected, she saw a total stranger. The feeling of loneliness was so great that for a moment Rosie was chilled, and could think of no words to say to this man who stood before her. She felt all over again how alone she was in this place, and how much danger she was in. She had to find Marie and then do what she could to find the watch that would be her way back to the future.

It was then that Rosie raised her head and saw the great platform in front of the palace, and the block where the King would lay his head for the axe-man to chop it off.

Mr Jones' film had seemed horrible at the time, but it was nothing to this. This was public, violent and deliberate death, and it was done in cold blood, for all the passion that had gone before it. Now, more than anything else, Rosie must find Marie, so neither of them had to see this alone.

She moved away from the crowd around her and started to search for the other girl, going this way and that. Twice she saw girls she thought might be Marie, and started towards them, only to find they were strangers when she came closer. She did not know what time it was, or what time they were going to bring the King from his prison, but the sun was getting high in the sky. Another couple of hours or so and it would be as high as it was going to get at this time of year. How long were they going to wait?

Even as Rosie wondered, there was a stir among those at the front of the crowd and she pushed her way forward. A murmur rose, and then one or two shouts. Far off, Rosie could hear the beat of drums.

When Rosie had at last got closer to the front, she found that she was taller than most of the women there, so she could see over their heads to the flutter of flags in the icy wind. She did not need to listen to the whispers in the crowd to know that these were the royal colours, and the soldiers marching towards them were bringing out the King and his last loyal men.

Rosie felt her stomach clench, and she found it was hard to breathe. Where was Marie? Was she close? Her father might be one of the men who was up there with the King!

She turned around again and knocked into someone. "I'm sorry," she said, only glancing at the woman she'd bumped. Then she stopped. Joy and pity and relief all welled up inside her. Marie's face was just the same as it was in the picture, except for the grief. That was so terrible that Rosie ached to do something about it, at the same time as she knew there was nothing anyone could do.

"Have you come to see your people's victory?" asked Marie.

Rosie felt her cheeks burn. "No." She held out the bread that Marie's cook had sent for her.

"What's that?" Marie asked.

"Bread," Rosie replied. "Your cook sent it for you. She said you went out without anything this morning."

Marie frowned at her, puzzled. "How do you know my cook?"

"My brother sent me to your house," said Rosie. She held out the watch in her other hand.

Marie took the watch and stared at it. There was an odd look on her face.

"I haven't seen David since Naseby," she said, after a moment. "Is he well?"

"He was hurt," Rosie told her. "He lost his leg and his arm is bad. But he'll be alright." She looked up and saw Marie close her eyes in horror. Then she opened them again and blinked a few times, took a deep breath and looked past Rosie. A cold, closed look came down over her face.

"Tell him I am glad to hear that he will recover," she said. "I know I will never see him again, but I will always think of him with kindness."

"Is that how it is?" Rosie cried. "You're going to leave him just because he's lost his leg? That's … That's horrible! I'm sorry I came for you now!"

Tears sprang into her eyes and she turned to go, but Marie grabbed her arm and stopped her.

"What do you mean?" she asked. "*David* has deserted *me*! I haven't heard one word from him since Naseby, and all of my letters have been sent back unopened."

Rosie saw her father's stern face in her mind and she felt her cheeks flush with anger.

"That will have been my parents," she said. "While David was too sick to know. But you must believe me when I tell you how much he loves you. He sent me today so that you wouldn't be alone. He thought your father might be walking with the King."

"He is."

Rosie swallowed. "It's going to be horrible," she said. "All this is horrible. Please forgive David. At least then there will be one thing this hasn't spoiled."

Marie nodded and took Rosie's hand. "There's nothing to forgive," she said. "Thank you."

As Marie spoke, the crowd around them fell silent. The soldiers walked with the King into the Palace of Whitehall.

"It's the end," one woman said, with a catch in her voice. Her face was very pale and there were shadows round her eyes. "England won't be England any more."

"Yes it will," Rosie said. "This won't last forever."

"But we can't bring the King back," the woman said, and shook her head.

"But Prince Charles escaped," Marie said.

"Yes," said Rosie. "And England will get tired of the Lord Protector one day. The time will come when people will want music and joy and colour again. Trust me, it won't be like this forever."

Marie looked at Rosie in amazement. "It's not safe to say such things here!" she warned, with fear in her voice. "What sort of Puritan are you?"

"One who has been turned against her own parents by all this," Rosie said. "And whatever the rights and wrongs of the King and the Lord Protector, that can't be right. Brother fighting brother, and daughters turned against their parents forever."

"No," said Marie. "None of it is right. They say the King took too much power for himself, but what is Cromwell doing by killing him? The same thing. He has won, but he has no grace or mercy. And that is what he said of the King!"

It was not much longer before the King was brought out of Whitehall onto the black draped platform where the axe and the block waited. He walked with several men, and the whole area was surrounded by many soldiers.

Rosie was startled. The King was a little man, no bigger than Rosie herself. He had a thick jacket on, or perhaps two, one over the other. He stood very straight. His sad face with its fine, dark eyes showed no fear at all. He looked once at the axe, and then away again. Rosie could not imagine what bravery that must have taken.

The King looked at the man beside him and began to speak. Because of the crowd it was possible to hear very little of what he said, even as close as Rosie and Marie were. His voice was quiet, and without anger, and it did not shake.

"I hope there is a good man here that will bear witness that I have forgiven all the world and even those that have been the cause of my death," he said. "Who they are God knows – I do not wish to know. I pray God that this may not be laid to their charge."

He spoke a little more, then turned to the man near him who gave him a white cap, which he put on. He paused and spoke to the Executioner. "Does my hair trouble you?" he asked.

The Executioner seemed to want all of his hair to be put up in the cap, and so with the Executioner's help, the King did so.

The man next to him, who seemed to be a priest of some sort, spoke to him in a low voice.

"You give up an earthly crown but you will have an eternal one now – a good exchange," the priest said.

Then the King took off his cloak and passed something to the priest, and stooping down, laid his neck on the block. After a tiny pause he stretched out his hands and the Executioner swung the axe, taking his head off with one blow.

Marie gasped and covered her face with her hands.

Rosie put her arms around her and held her, feeling her body shake as she sobbed. She did it for Marie, and her grief; but she needed the hug for herself too. There was a horror to what she had seen that she would never forget. A living man, brave and stubborn, had in an instant become a bleeding, headless corpse. And it was no awful accident, but something done in public and on purpose, while thousands of his followers looked on. Rosie was not a Puritan or a Royalist, but a human being, cold and frightened at this awful act.

"Come home," she said to Marie. "Come away from here."

Marie said nothing, but she allowed Rosie to lead her away from the crowd. Some others were trying to leave too. Many more pressing to the front to dip hankies in the King's blood. Perhaps they wanted something to remember him by. Or perhaps they wanted to prove to themselves that he was really dead.

Chapter 8
Goodness

As they walked away from Whitehall, Rosie kept her arm around Marie to stop her being bumped or knocked by the other people leaving. At last they reached an empty street where they could walk without being pushed or shoved.

Marie walked in silence, lost in her own thoughts. Rosie tried to think of something to say that would comfort her, but it was hard to get it all straight in her own mind. The Civil War was over and Marie's side had lost. The King was dead and his sons were in exile, who knew where? David had said the Queen was in France, so maybe the King's sons were there too. Rosie knew that Cromwell wouldn't be Lord Protector for ever, but she didn't know how long it would be till things changed, or what would come after.

"Why did your family like the King?" she asked Marie.

Marie stopped and looked at her.

"You must have a reason," Rosie said. "David said you were prepared to stand up for him, even die for him."

Marie looked down at the ground, her face red. "I don't know if we do love the King so much. Perhaps ... perhaps we're just afraid of Cromwell."

Rosie thought of Praisegod Barebones, the man who had come into the tailor's shop. Her Puritan father loved him, and she knew that her parents would say he was a good man. But what did it mean to be good? Did it mean you had to be miserable and afraid? Couldn't you be good and happy as well?

"What do you think it means, to be good?" she asked Marie.

"I don't know," Marie said. "It must mean more than just wearing dark clothes and being quiet and grave all the time. I think you can follow all those rules, and think about God all the time, and still be unkind to other people."

"I think being good means thinking about other people instead of yourself," Rosie said. "That's all I can think of."

All of a sudden, Marie smiled. It changed her face, making her beautiful.

"So you are good," she said. "Because you came to help me in order to help your brother. And so is David, who must have been in such pain that he could hardly bear it, but who still thought of me more than he thought of himself."

"I think that's because he loves you," Rosie said. "So what will happen now? I mean, what will you and David do?"

Marie's mouth set in a determined line. "I will tell my father I wish to marry him."

"What about my parents?" Rosie asked.

"My father is a rich man," Marie said. "He can provide for both of us. We don't need your parents to agree."

"That will be hard for David," Rosie said. "To hurt them like that."

"Well, then I must hurt my father," Marie said. "I will leave his house, leave all his money and my fine silks and lace and live as a Puritan. I would do that, if only I could have David."

Rosie smiled. "I am so glad you have found each other again."

"And I have found a sister," Marie said, and kissed Rosie on the cheek. She put something in Rosie's hand. "Take this to David for me."

Rosie did not need to look to see what it was Marie had given her, but still she opened her hand. The gold of the little watch in her palm winked in the chilly sun. Cold as the day was, it glowed with warmth in Rosie's hand. She opened the case and saw it was the match of the watch David had given her that morning. That one held a picture of Marie, and this held a picture of David.

"Go now," Marie said to her. "Tell David that I will come later today to bring him to my father's house. And if my father will not take him, or David will not come, then I will do what I must. I will go with David to church and never return to my father's house again."

Rosie kissed Marie on her cheek, and they went their separate ways.

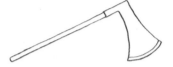

Chapter 9
Home Truths

The morning after Marie and David's wedding, Rosie was not surprised to wake up in a very different room – her own room at home, with its TV and posters and rugs and knick-knacks. With the little gold watch clasped in her hand, she lay in bed for a few moments and thought about all the things that had happened over the last few days.

Marie had been as good as her word. The very night Marie met Rosie, she and her father had come to Rosie's family home and told her parents that Marie and David wanted to marry.

Marie's father would take them both into his own home and look after them as long as he lived. He would leave them everything when he died.

After the first shock, David and Rosie's parents were not so angry as Rosie had expected. She realised that they had in fact been very worried about David and his future. With one bad arm there was no way he could take over the family business when his father died, and they were not rich enough to leave him what money he would need once they were gone.

Their father and Marie's father went off into the other room to talk while the others held their breath outside. When they came back out again, everything was settled. Marie and David would be married the very next day.

That night, David told Rosie that Marie's father and their father had been friends when they were young. It was hard for Rosie to believe this, but then she remembered again the way that the Civil War had torn families apart. Little wonder if friendships died, in a world where parents would not speak to their own children.

Back in the present, it was Saturday, so Rosie took her time getting ready. When she had eaten, she got out her history things and made a start on her homework. Mr Jones had asked them to write a play about the two sides in the Civil War. That would need no leaps of the imagination for Rosie! She decided that she would write the story of Marie and David.

Rosie had nearly finished her first try at a script when she heard the door-bell ring. A moment later, her mother came to her bedroom door.

"There's someone here to see you, love," she said. "It's your friend Zack."

Rosie sat up, her heart pounding. "Let him in," she said.

Rosie's mother showed Zack into the room and then went off down the stairs. Zack didn't come right in, but stood in the door and looked at Rosie with an uncertain smile on his face.

"Do you want to see me?" he asked.

"Of course," Rosie said, and before she knew it she had jumped up and thrown herself at him. Zack got his arms up just in time to catch her before she knocked them both onto the floor.

"I'm sorry," she said, her voice muffled by his t-shirt.

"I'm sorry, too," Zack said, and kissed her hair. "I was going mental last night when you didn't answer your phone. I thought you were still angry with me."

"Of course not," Rosie said. "I fell asleep, that's all."

"Fell asleep?" Zack pretended to look hurt. "I was going out of my mind and you were *asleep?*"

Rosie's cheeks went red. "I cried so much I tired myself out," she confessed.

Zack let her go, and sat down on the rug beside all Rosie's papers and books. He stretched out a hand to her. "Why don't you come here and tell me all about it?" he asked.

So Rosie told him everything about how she had been left behind as all of her friends learned to read and words and letters still made no sense to her at all. She told him about how she'd made friends with Stacey so no one would pick on her and how she'd made a pain of herself in class so the teachers would think she was just a bad pupil. She showed him the script she had written for History.

"See?" she said. "I can't spell at all."

Zack stroked her arm as he read the script. "This is good, Rosie," he said.

Rosie went red again. "But it's such a mess. Can you even read it?"

"OK, the spelling's a mess, but the writing's good," Zack told her. "And who cares about spelling? You can get a computer to do that for you now." He looked up from the paper. "Is this girl called Rose based on you, Rosie? The Puritan girl?"

"Yes," Rosie said. "And the others are all real people, too. Look." She handed him the watch. "This is a portrait of David," she said. "Before he lost his leg at Naseby."

"Wow," Zack said, as he stared at the tiny painting. "This must be worth a fortune." He looked at Rosie with a frown. "Hang on a minute! You had that watch that belonged to Edith Cavell as well. Are you some kind of antique watch thief, Rosie?"

Rosie smiled at him. "No! But I do have a friend who is a sort of ... collector. In fact, I'd like you to meet him. If I tell you about his watches, I don't think you'd believe me. I'll have to let him tell you himself."

"Later on," Zack said, and pulled her to him. "Right now, I'm happy right where I am."

"Me too," said Rosie. "Me too."

Our books are tested
for children and young people by
children and young people.

Thanks to everyone who consulted on
a manuscript for their time and effort in
helping us to make our books better
for our readers.

Other titles in the Timepiece series *by Anne Perry...*

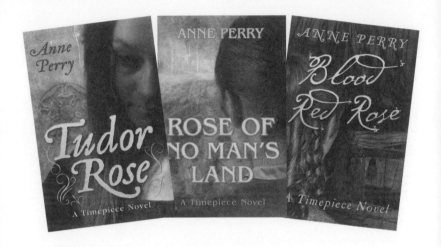

Tudor Rose

2011. *Rosie Sands knows she's making the wrong choices in life,but it's tough when you're 15 and you can't even read.*

1588. *Elizabeth Tudor must face the enemy fleet gathering in the English Channel, but she knows there is danger on every side.*

When Rosie finds a very special watch in her school bag, four hundred years of history disappear to bring her face to face with Elizabeth. A great Queen and a troubled school-girl find they can help each other in ways no one could have imagined...

Rose of No Man's Land

2011. *Rosie Sands can't trust anyone enough to admit she has a problem. Not her parents, or her teachers, and especially not Zack Edwards, the coolest boy in school.*

1915. *Nurse Edith Cavell must put her own life in danger as she helps British soldiers to escape from Belgium under the noses of the Germans. Every day could be her last.*

When Rosie is given a WWI nurse's watch and wakes up in Edith Cavell's hospital, she finds herself surrounded by secrets and lies. Does she dare to get involved, or is it easier to look the other way?

Blood Red Rose

2012. *Rosie Sands is determined her boyfriend Zack won't find out she can't read, but it's tough when he keeps asking for help with his charity work for the Third World.*

1812. *The captain of The Red Rose must take his ship across a vast ocean, but it's terrifying when the illegal cargo in the hold means that every other ship could be an enemy.*

When Rosie wakes up one morning on board *The Red Rose*, she faces the greatest danger of her life. The weather is wild, the crew is blind and most of the people below decks have no reason to want to help...